Tree Wise

The Signing Branches

By

Antoinette Abbamonte

Illustrated by

Heng Bee Tan

Strategic Book Publishing and Rights Co.

Book Design/Layout by Kalpart. Visit www.kalpart.com

Strategic Book Publishing and Rights Co.
12620 FM 1960, Suite A4-507
Houston, TX 77065
www.sbpra.com

**For information about special discounts for bulk purchases,
please contact Strategic Book Publishing and Rights Co. Special Sales,
at bookorder@sbpra.net.**

ISBN: 978-1-62857-646-7

Paule Verdier

Thank you for your continued love and encouragement.

Austin, Brock, Dylan, and Jaden

Thank you so much for your effort to adopt a new language and culture.

I love you!

This delightful book tells the story of a boy who has parents who are deaf and has become friends with a girl at school. Through the help of a very special tree, the boy learns how to help his new friend and classmates understand more about deaf culture. The tree teaches sign language to the children through games. The pictures are very colorful and make it easy to pick up sign language.

It was Reed's first day of kindergarten. His mom was driving and it was a bright and sunny day. When Reed got out of the car, in front of his new school, he said goodbye to his mom, and she told him she would pick him up when school was over: They were talking, but they were also moving their hands, and Reed's mother's voice sounded strange.

A lot of the kids were walking into the school, but one girl, Paige, stopped and looked at Reed and his mom waving their hands around. She heard his mom's voice, and couldn't understand it.

When it was time for recess, all of the kids went into the schoolyard to play on the swings, slide, and monkey bars.

Paige walked up to Reed and said, "My name is Paige. What's your name?"

"Hi, I'm Reed. How are you? I really like our teacher. She's a nice lady," Reed replied.

"Why does your mom's voice sound funny? And why do you move your hands when you talk to her?" Paige asked.

Reed started to blush. He was embarrassed. He turned away from Paige and ran to the line of trees in the back of the schoolyard. He sat down in the shade under a big apple tree and hung his head. Just then, an apple fell down and hit him on top of his head!

"Ouch! Hey, you, that wasn't very nice!" Reed said, looking up into the big leaves and long branches.

"I'm sorry," said the tree, much to Reed's surprise. "I just wanted to say 'hello' because you look so sad."

"You can talk?" Reed asked, staring at the tree trunk.

There, he saw a face! And the face was smiling!

"Yes, and I can also talk with my hands!" The tree's branches stretched out in front of Reed. "Can I help you?" asked the tree.

"I feel bad because Paige said that my mom's voice sounds funny," said Reed.

"Well, you could explain to Paige that your mom can't hear her voice and that's why it sounded differently. Maybe you can help Paige understand," said the tree.

Just then Reed heard the school bell ring. That meant it was time to go back into the class.

"Thanks a lot!" said Reed. "Can I come talk with you again tomorrow?"

"I would like that!" said the tree, waving goodbye. "What's your name?"

"I'm Reed," and with that, he ran back into school.

When the bell sounded and the school day was over, Reed went outside with all of the other kids to wait for his mom. He saw Paige and remembered what the tree had said.

He walked over to Paige and said, "My mom is deaf. That means that she can't hear, and that's why her voice sounds different."

"How can you talk to your mom if she can't hear?" asked Paige.

"My mom watches my facial expressions when I talk and I use my hands to make words. It's called sign language."

"That's really neat!" said Paige.

Just then, Reed saw his mom's car pull up.

"My mom's here now. I will see you tomorrow," Reed said, turning to go to the car.

"Is it okay if I meet your mom?" asked Paige.

"Okay, come with me," said Reed.

The children walked over to the car and Reed's mom got out to help him into the back seat.

"Hi, Mom. This is my new friend, Paige," said Reed, while using his hands to make words.

"Hi, Paige! Nice to meet you!" said Reed's mom.

"Reed, tell your mom that I say it's nice to meet her, too," said Paige, shyly, looking at the ground.

Reed used his hands to tell his mom what Paige had said. His mom smiled and helped Reed into the car.

They both waved as they drove away.

The next day at recess, Reed went to see the tree again.

"Hello? Can I talk to you?" asked Reed, looking up at the big tree.

"Hello, Reed! It's nice to see you again!"

"I have a question. When Paige was talking to my mom, why didn't she look into my mom's eyes?" Reed asked.

"Sometimes people who can hear don't realize how important it is to deaf people to look into their eyes when they are talking. Paige probably didn't understand. You can help her try to communicate with deaf people, like your mom, in a better way," said the tree.

"Okay, I will talk to her, but how?" asked Reed.

"Show Paige how you talk with your mom. Tell her that it's important for her to look into the eyes of a deaf person when talking to them so that they know you are talking to them and not someone else."

"Yeah! Now I feel better! I will help Paige!" Reed said, excitedly.

"Yes, you can help Paige and other people do lots of things! Many people have never met a deaf person and they don't know these things. You can help them," said the tree, with a smile.

When school was over for the day, Reed found Paige outside, waiting for her mom.

"Reed! Is your mom coming to pick you up again?"

"Yes, she will be here soon," said Reed.

"Can you show me how to talk with my hands so I can say 'hello'?"

Reed was excited! He showed Paige the sign for 'hello'.

"And this is how you say, 'Nice to meet you'."

"Wow! I can talk with my hands! I can't wait to show your mom!" said Paige, jumping up and down.

"When you talk with your hands, it's important to look into the eyes of the person you're talking to. That way they'll know you're talking to them," said Reed.

"Okay! That makes sense!" Paige said.

Reed was so happy that Paige wanted to learn about sign language. And Paige was excited to try out her new skill. When Reed's mom pulled up in the car, both children ran over to it, with big smiles on their faces.

"Hello! Nice to meet you!" said Paige, while signing.

Reed's mother's eyes lit up. She was surprised!

"Nice to meet you, too!"

"I want to learn more! Will you help me?" Paige asked.

"Sure! I'll see you tomorrow!" said Reed, as he got into the car.

The next day, Reed and Paige sat outside during recess and Reed told Paige about a special alphabet just for hands.

"You can make all the letters with your hands. That's a good place to start learning. I will show you."

Reed and Paige went through all the letters, and then practiced them until the bell rang, telling them to come back in to class.

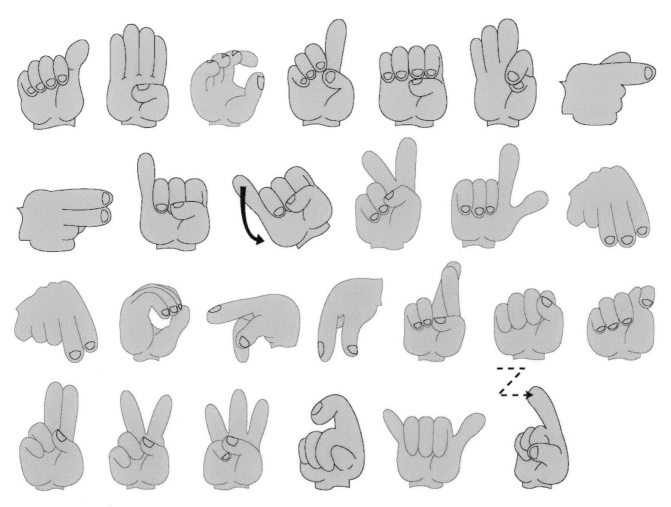

When school let out, Reed and Paige walked to the cars.

"Reed, maybe tomorrow you can teach me more words!" said Paige.

"Maybe you can come to my house! We can play and I'll show you more sign language!" Reed said. "I'll ask my mom."

Reed signed to his mother and she started nodding her head.

"My mom says, if it's okay with your mom, you can come to my house tomorrow after school," said Reed.

"OKAY! I will ask my mom! See you tomorrow!" said Paige, waving goodbye.

The next day, after school, Paige was excited to go to Reed's house. When they arrived, the house looked like hers, but there were some different things inside. The first thing she saw was a phone with something that looked like a typewriter on it.

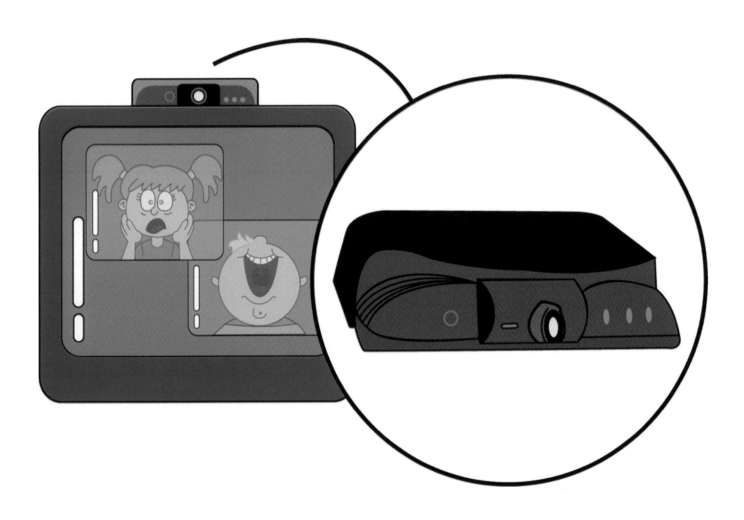

"What's that?" Paige asked Reed.

"That's the phone that my mom uses. She doesn't hear, so she types what she wants to say and what the other people say shows up on that screen," and Reed pointed to the phone.

"Oh, that's neat!"

"We have a new phone, too. I like to play with it. Do you want to see it?"

"Okay!"

And with that, Reed and Paige went into another room. Paige did not see a phone, only a TV with something on top of it.

"I don't see a phone."

"The TV is the phone! Look. I'll show you!" Reed pushed some buttons and then Reed and Paige were looking at themselves on the TV!

"Wow! I've never been on TV before! But how do you use it like a phone?" Paige asked.

"My mom calls other people with the same kind of TV. Then, they can see each other and use sign language. It's a lot of fun, too. I get to see my grandma on the TV and she lives really far away!" explained Reed.

Reed and Paige made some funny faces and danced around, watching themselves on the TV.

All of a sudden, Paige heard a loud BANG!

"What was that?" Paige asked.

"Oh, my mom is in the kitchen, making dinner. Sometimes she closes the cabinets too hard, but she doesn't mean to scare you. She doesn't hear the loud noise."

"So does your mom ever tell you to be quiet when you're playing?" asked Paige.

"No! I can be as loud as I want!"

Reed and Paige spent the rest of the afternoon playing. They were having a great time. They started coloring, and Reed thought about what the tree had said about teaching Paige.

"Do you want to learn some more signs, Paige?"

"Okay! My favorite color is blue. How do you make that sign?"

Reed showed Paige the sign for 'blue'.

"Oh, it looks like the letter 'B'. I can do that!"

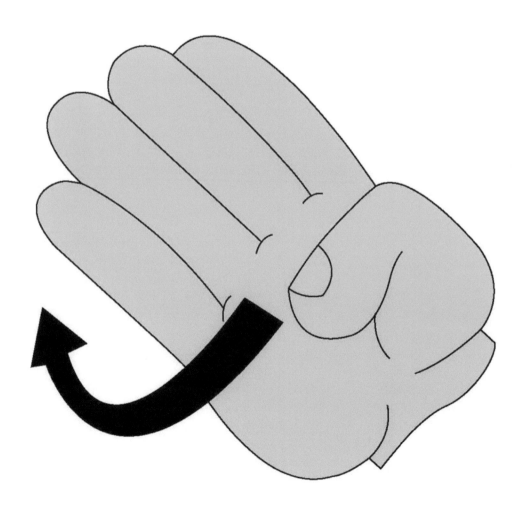

"What about yellow, green, and pink?" Paige asked excitedly.

Reed showed her some of the colors that he thought would be easy to learn.

He chose signs that look like the letters they start with.

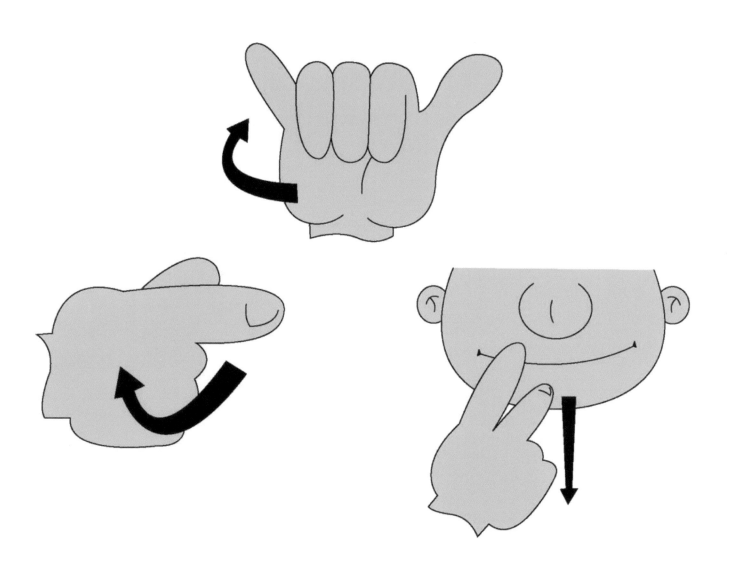

"What about 'car'? You drew a car and a boy and a dog. How do you make all those signs?" Paige asked.

Reed was excited that Paige wanted to learn. He showed her the signs for 'car', 'boy', 'dog', 'cat', and 'girl'.

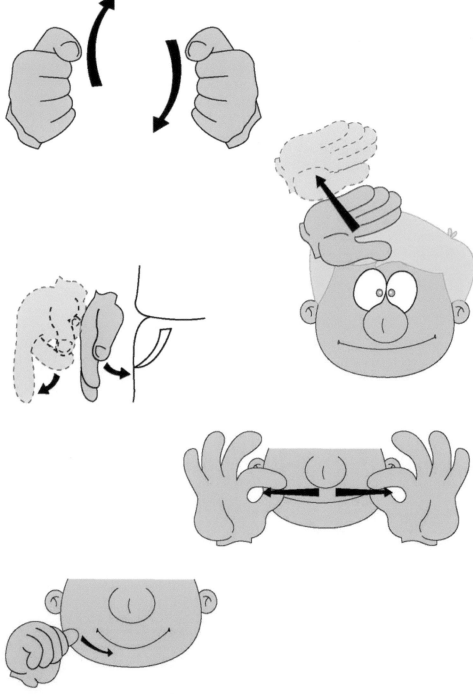

"See, 'car' looks like you're driving, 'boy' is like holding a baseball cap, 'dog' is like calling your dog to come here, and 'cat' looks like whiskers," Reed explained.

"What about 'girl'? Why does it look like that?" Paige wondered.

"My mom says that it looks like you're putting on a scarf or a bonnet, like girls used to wear a long time ago. Sometimes signs don't make sense, but it's easier to start learning with the ones that do."

Just then, Paige heard a doorbell and the lights in the room started to flash.

"Why are the lights turning on and off?" asked Paige.

"When the doorbell rings, the lights flash so that my mom will know that there is someone at the door," explained Reed.

Reed's mother and Paige's mother walked into the room. It was time for Paige to go home.

"Thanks a lot! I had a lot of fun today! I'll see you at school tomorrow!" said Paige as she waved goodbye to Reed and his mom.

At recess the next day, Reed decided to introduce Paige to the tree.

"I want you to meet my other friend! He's very smart and he helps me a lot," said Reed as they walked into the schoolyard.

"That's him!" said Reed, pointing to the big apple tree.

"A tree is your friend? How can that be?" Paige looked at Reed with wide eyes.

"It's true!" said a loud deep voice. Paige looked up at the tree and saw that he was looking down at her!

"Wow! Hi! I'm Paige!"

"It's very nice to meet you, Paige," said the tree. "I hear Reed has been teaching you about sign language."

"Yes, he has! I'm learning so much! Do you know sign language?" asked Paige.

"He sure does! Isn't that neat?" said Reed.

"We should tell all of the other kids about the tree! I bet they would think that was really cool! And then, we could teach them about sign language, too!" suggested Paige.

"What a great idea!" said the tree. "I know just how to get their attention. Watch this!"

All of a sudden, a bunch of pretty colorful butterflies came out of the tree's branches and flew over to the rest of the kids playing outside. The butterflies paused for a moment while the kids stared at them with their mouths open.

"Come on! Let's follow them!" said one of the kids.

The kids ran across the schoolyard and stopped when they got to the tree.

"Hello!" said the tree.

The kids were a little scared, until the tree brought his branches down and started tickling them.

The tree also dropped a few apples onto some of the kids' heads, just to tease.

Reed, Paige, and all of their classmates started laughing, and so did the tree.

"Okay! That's enough! Let's all play a game!" said Reed.

"I know the perfect game to play! Let's play Simon Says!" said the tree. "At the same time, you can all learn some sign language!"

All the children cheered and got ready to play.

"Okay! Ready? Simon says BOOK!" and the tree signed the word BOOK.

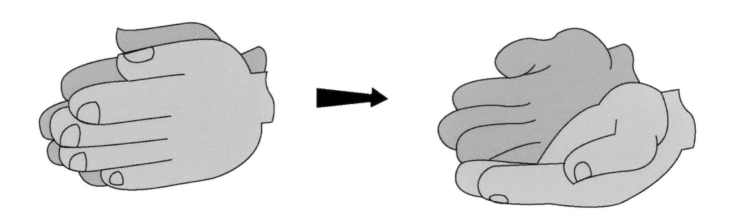

All the children made books with their hands.
"Good! Now, Simon says BUTTERFLY!"

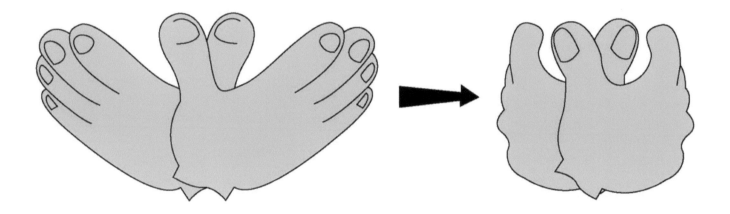

All the children made the sign for butterfly with their hands. "Simon says SCHOOL!"

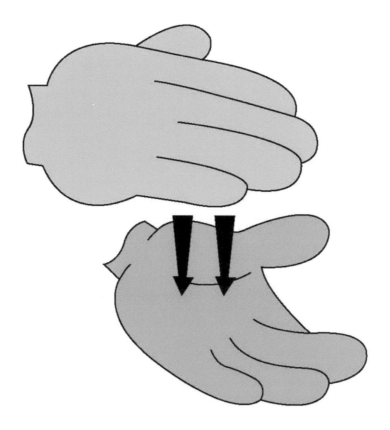

All the children signed school.

"ICE CREAM!" said the tree.

None of the children signed ice cream. "Very good! You didn't make the sign because I didn't say Simon says! Okay! Last one! Simon says TREE!" said the tree.

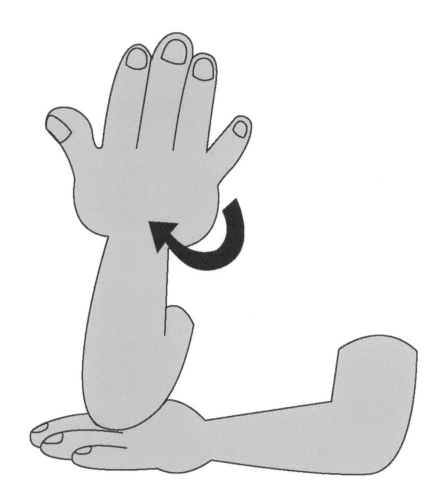

All the children signed tree. At that moment, the bell rang and the teacher came out to find the children. The tree suddenly became very still.

"Hey! What happened to the tree? He's not talking anymore!" said one of the children.

"Maybe he only talks to kids!" suggested Paige.

"I think you're right!" said Reed.

"Children! It's time to come back to class!" the teacher shouted out.

The kids all waved to the tree, even though the tree did not wave back.

"We will see you tomorrow and learn more sign language!" said Paige.

"Yay!" exclaimed the children, and they ran back to school. The tree waited for them.

Review Requested:

If you loved this book, would you please provide a review at Amazon.com?

Thank You

CPSIA information can be obtained at www.ICGtesting.com
Printed in the USA
BVIW12n1729050515
398976BV00001B/1